Hanna Hippo's Horrible Hiccups

by Barbara deRubertis • illustrated by R.W. Alley

THE KANE PRESS / NEW YORK

Alpha Betty's Class

Alexander Anteater

Bobby Baboon

Corky Cub

Dilly Dog

STAR of the BOOK

Eddie Elephant

Frances Frog

Gertie Gorilla

Hanna Hippo

Lana Llama

Izzy Impala

Jeremy Jackrabbit

Kylie Kangaroo

Maxwell Moose

Library of Congress Cataloging-in-Publication Data

deRubertis, Barbara.
Hanna Hippo's horrible hiccups / by Barbara deRubertis ; illustrated by R.W. Alley.
p. cm. — (Animal antics A to Z)
Summary: When Hanna Hippo gets hiccups on her way to enjoy some hot huckleberry muffins
after school, her friends Homer Hog and Hilda Hen try to help.
ISBN 978-1-57565-319-8 (library binding : alk. paper) — ISBN 978-1-57565-312-9 (pbk. : alk. paper)
[1. Hiccups—Fiction. 2. Hippopotamus—Fiction. 3. Hogs—Fiction. 4. Chickens—Fiction.
5. Alphabet. 6. Humorous stories.] I. Alley, R. W. (Robert W.), ill. II. Title.
PZ7.D4475Han 2010
[E]—dc22   2009049883

1 3 5 7 9 10 8 6 4 2

First published in the United States of America in 2010 by Kane Press, Inc.
Printed in the United States of America
WOZ0710

Series Editor: Juliana Hanford
Book Design: Edward Miller

Animal Antics A to Z is a registered trademark of Kane Press, Inc.

www.kanepress.com

Hanna Hippo was humming a happy tune as she left Alpha Betty's school.

She was hoping to have a heap of Homer Hog's heavenly huckleberry muffins.

Hanna was a happy hippo.

But, like all hippos, she was hungry
at the end of the day. VERY hungry.

HILL
STREET

And nothing made her tummy happier
than those huckleberry muffins.

Hanna saw Homer Hog's Bakery
at the top of the hill ahead.

"Hi, ho! Hum de dum!
Hippity hop! Here I come!"
Hanna hollered.

Hanna happily began to hop up the hill.

Soon she was huffing and puffing.

It was a HIGH hill!

Hanna hauled her heavy feet higher and higher. "This is hard work!" she said.

But the hope of having Homer Hog's heavenly huckleberry muffins helped her along.

"Here I come, Homer!" she hollered ahead.

Homer hollered back, "Hurry, Hanna!
Have some huckleberry muffins
while they're hot!"

11

That was just what Hanna needed to hear.

She hustled right to the top of that hill.

Hanna was very happy to see Homer!
She gave him a huge hippo hug.

"Hi, Homer!" she said.

"I'll have a . . . *HIC.*

HIC . . . HIC . . . HIC!"

"Oh, nooooo!" said Hanna unhappily.

"I have hiccups!
HIC . . . HIC . . . HIC!

I can't eat huckleberry muffins while
I have hiccups!"

"How horrible, Hanna!" said Homer.
"Try holding your breath!"

Hanna held her breath.

Then she hiccupped again.

"HIC!"

"Hold your breath and hop up and
down!" said Homer.

Hanna held her breath.
She hopped up and down.

And then she hiccupped AGAIN.

Hanna howled. "Please help me, Homer!"

"Here," said Homer.
"Have a hot cup of tea with honey."

Hanna held the cup of tea.

She had a sip.
She had another sip.
She had still another sip.

And then Hanna hiccupped
harder than ever.

"HIC!"

Hanna was very unhappy.
And VERY hungry!

She tried to hide her huge tears
from Homer.

Suddenly, she heard a humongous . . .

"SQUAWK!"

Hanna hopped high
in the sky.

"Hoppin' hippos!" Hanna hollered.
"What was THAT?"

"Hi, Hanna!" said Hilda Hen.
"I heard your hiccups.
So I hurried over to help!"

"You gave me a horrible SCARE, Hilda!"
said Hanna.

"But, Hanna!" said Homer.

"That horrible scare must have helped.
I don't hear any more hiccups!"

Homer
Hog's
Bakery

"You're right!" said Hanna happily.

And she gave Hilda Hen a huge hippo hug.

"Hilda!" said Hanna. "Let's both have some of Homer's huckleberry muffins!"

"Oh, happy day!" said Hilda.

Homer handed them a plate of hot muffins.
They looked absolutely heavenly.

"Thank you, Homer!" said Hilda.
"Thank you, Homer!" said Hanna.

And Homer said,

"HIC!"

FUN FACTS

- Home: Africa, south of the Sahara Desert
- Size: The common hippopotamus, or hippo, is one of the heaviest land animals. It weighs around 7,000 pounds!
- Food: With their huge mouths and teeth, hippos can gobble up to 100 pounds of plants in one night!
- Homes: During the day hippos hang out in mud or stay underwater to keep cool, but they must come up to breathe every five minutes or so.
- **Did You Know?** When they are threatened, hippos are one of the most ferocious of all animals . . . and they can outrun a human! Look out!

LOOK BACK

Learning to identify letter sounds (phonemes) at the beginning, middle, and end of words is called "phonemic awareness."

- The word *hop* <u>begins</u> with the *h* sound. Listen to the words on page 5 being read again. When you hear a word that <u>begins</u> with the *h* sound, hop on one foot. When you hear the next *h* sound, hop onto the other foot.
- Now listen to the words on pages 6–7 being read again. Every time you hear the *h* sound at the <u>beginning</u> of a word, hold up a finger. How many fingers are you holding up after listening to these pages?

TRY THIS!

Hop to the top of the hill for a huckleberry muffin!

- Place five numbered pieces of paper in a line across the floor. On paper #5, draw a picture of a huckleberry muffin. This is the "top of the hill"!
- Stand in front of paper #1, and listen to the words in the box below being read aloud, one at a time.
- When you hear a word that begins with the *h* sound, hop forward one space. If the word does NOT begin with the *h* sound, hop back a space. (Hop beside the pieces of paper, not *on* them.)

hog happy dog hug hop hungry
bug top hill huff hippo

Did you make it to the muffin? If not, start over and try again!

FOR MORE ACTIVITIES, go to Hanna Hippo's website: www.kanepress.com/AnimalAntics/HannaHippo.html
You'll also find a recipe for Homer Hog's Huckleberry Muffins!